JUST PLAIN BOB

Watching
my shared
Wife

WARNING

This book contains sexually explicit scenes and adult language. It may be considered offensive to some readers. This book is for sale to adults ONLY.

* * * * * * * * * * * * * * * * * * * *

Please store your files wisely where they cannot be accessed by underage readers.

Please feel free to send me an email. Just know that these emails are filtered by my publisher. Good news is always welcome.

Just Plain Bob - **justplainbob@awesomeauthors.org**

About the Publisher

4Fun Publishing, a member of **BLVNP Incorporated**, 340 S. Lemon #6200, Walnut CA 91789, info@blvnp.com / legal@blvnp.com
NOTE: Due to the highly emotional reaction of some people to works of erotic fiction, any email sent to the above address that contains foul language or religious references is automatically deleted by our anti-spam software and will not be seen. All other communications are welcome.

DISCLAIMER

Please don't be stupid and kill yourself. This book is a work of FICTION. Do not try any new sexual practice that you find in this book. It is fiction and not to be confused with reality. Neither the author nor the publisher or its associates assume any responsibility for any loss, injury, death or legal consequences resulting from acting on the contents in this book. Every character in this book is over 18 years of age. The author's opinions are not to be construed as the opinions of the publisher. The material in this book is for entertainment purposes ONLY. Enjoy.

Rob is a hardworking, faithful and loving husband to Mandy. His erratic work schedule oftentimes keeps him from sleeping with his wife at nights.

One day, while fixing his garden, he stumbles into something unusual that's being set up inside his home. He asks a friend to help him figure out what the complicated surveillance gadgets installed around the house is for.

Then, he discovers that his wife is not what she seems to be...

Watching
My Shared Wife

By: Just Plain Bob

ISBN: 978-1-68030-004-8

God alone knows how long it might have gone on if it hadn't been for the ants. I didn't know it was ants -- I thought it was termites.

There was a row of bushes across the front of the house and right up against it and for ten years I had done nothing to them but trim them. One day I noticed that the head patterns of the sprinkler heads in the front yard seemed to be weak and figuring that I had a leak in the system I went looking for it. There was one head under the bushes and I got down and pushed the bushes out of the way to look at it. I noticed that the wood trim around the base of the house looked rotten and I ran a fingernail across it and a large chunk just fell away exposing what looked like burrows or little tunnels. Shit! Termites!

I finished checking the sprinkler heads and found one that the ground seemed soft around and then I noticed the indentation in the head. It looked as if one of the tines on the machine they used to aerate the yard had hit on the head. I dug around it and found that the connection between the PVC pipe and the riser was cracked. I repaired it, tested the system and saw that I now had good spray patterns. I put my tools away, had lunch and then started checking out the rest of the house for termites.

I was down in the basement pulling down insulation and checking the sill plates when I found it. (Sill plates are what they call the wood on top of the concrete wall of the basement - it is the transition point between the basement and the framing of the house.) It was a little black box about six inches, by four inches and was about three inches thick. It had a small on/off switch on one side and a glowing green light on the front and it was attached to the phone line.

I stood there on the ladder and stared at it. I had read enough spy novels and seen enough movies and TV shows to suspect that what I was looking at was a phone tap, but the thought seemed ridiculous. Who in the hell would be tapping my phone? Who would be interested in the phone conversations of an aircraft mechanic? Or those of a secretary which is what my wife Amanda was.

I carefully put everything back where I found it and then went upstairs to use the phone to call Terminex and set up an appointment for them to come out and look at my termite problem. Then I got in my car and drove to the 7-11 about eight miles from the house and used the pay phone to call a friend. Hal was an avionics tech I worked with and he ran a small electronics business on the side. I told him what I had found and he agreed to come look at it the next day.

That night when Mandy got home I had dinner ready and while we ate I debated telling her about what I'd found, but decided not to since she was by nature a worrier. I decided to wait until I had more information before telling her about it.

Another factor in my decision was that this was our hard time of the year. The airline I worked for had rotating shifts; four months of midnights, four months of afternoons and four months of days. I was in the last quarter of my graveyard turn, eleven-thirty at night until eight in the morning, and the grave shift was hard on us. Days was always good and swing shift - three to eleven-thirty - wasn't bad because I was always home at night to sleep with Mandy and be there in the morning when she woke up, but graves was the killer. We only saw each other from the time she got home around six-thirty until I had to leave for work at ten forty-five and she would already be gone to work when I got home in the morning. It was always a bad time for us, but the pay was very good, the benefits superb and you just could not beat the airline pass privileges. Still, she spent four months a year alone in bed and it wasn't easy on her. No sense in giving her something to worry about as she lay in that bed alone trying to sleep.

~~***~~

The next morning Hal followed me home and I showed him the small black box. He told me that it was a 'broadcast' sending unit and that it transmitted what it heard to a receiver.

"It only has a range of about three hundred yards."

"What does that mean?"

"It means that the unit it is sending to has to be fairly close to here. You've seen any strange vans or vehicles parked close by lately?"

"None that I'm aware of."

"You get along okay with your neighbors?"

"No problems with any of them in the nine years I've been here. Why?"

"The receiving unit has to be somewhere close. If there are no strange cars in the neighborhood then it has to be either in a neighbor's house or garage or right here in this house. Any place in the house that you never go?"

"Not that I can think of. I don't spend a lot of time in either of the spare bedrooms, but I do occasionally go into them."

"Let's go look at them."

We were in the closet of one of the spare bedrooms when he pointed up at the ceiling and asked, "What's that?"

I looked up and saw the hatch into the attic and told him what it was.

"Go up much?"

"Last time was maybe six years ago. I went up and put insulation batts down on top of the blown in insulation and then planked over them. I was going to use the area for storage, but it was a pain trying to move things up through that two foot by two foot hole so I gave up on the idea."

"Let's take a look up there."

I kept an eight foot fiberglass ladder in the upstairs utility closet for changing light bulbs and cleaning the blades of the ceiling fan in the master bedroom and I went and got it and we went up into the attic. I saw it as soon as my head went through the hatch. It looked like a laptop computer sitting on the planking. I pulled myself up into the attic and Hal followed me. As soon as he saw the device he said:

"Sweet fucking Jesus!"

"You know what it is?"

He walked over to it, knelt down and took a close look at it. "I've never seen one before, but I've read about them. Completely digital, lithium battery operated and stores up to one hundred and twenty hours of digital audio and visual. The battery is supposed to last three hundred hours. It has a small screen for viewing and has USB ports you can connect to download audio and video onto CDs or DVDs. This brings up a major question. What kind of serious shit are you and your wife into?"

"Nothing that I know of. Why?"

"Because this thing costs around twenty thousand dollars and to the best of my knowledge only the government has them. But even more serious is what this means to you."

"What do you mean by that?"

"Who knows that you never come up here? Who knows you keep a ladder in the utility closet? Who has access when you aren't home?"

I was stunned by the implications of what he'd just said. There was only one answer and that was my wife Mandy. Hal saw it sink in and said:

"Sorry Rob."

All I could do was shrug my shoulders as I tried to get my mind around all that it meant.

"Let's take a look through the rest of the house, but first let me see if I can disable this thing."

He picked it up, took a real close look at it and pushed on something and the battery pack slid out. He set it aside and said:

"Now it won't record everything we do."

It took a little over two hours to go through the house and Hal found eight battery operated mini cams that recorded audio and visual. He kept saying "Wow" every time he found one.

"These are state of the art Rob. There is a good thirty to thirty-five grand worth of stuff here."

There were two in the living room, one each in the dining room and family room, one in my basement workshop and three in the master bedroom. I asked him if he could help me try and find out what was going on and he said he would try.

The next morning while Hal was doing some work in the house the man from Terminex showed up and checked out the house. Turns out that it was carpenter ants instead of termites. He outlined a program for getting rid of them and keeping them away and I signed up and he left.

The first thing that Hal did when he got to the house was go up into the attic and take the battery out of the receiving unit so none of the cameras would record him as he went to work. He put a recorder on the phone lines and then set up voice activated tape recorders and mini cams in the bedroom and living room. Then he placed a mini cam in a corner of the attic and aimed it to cover the receiver.

The last thing he did was check out my pick-up truck. He found a GPS locator inside the rear frame in a place where I would never spot it unless I happened to walk under it while it was up on a hoist getting a grease job or an oil change and even then it wasn't likely that I would spot it unless I was looking for it.

He also found a voice activated tape recorder under my seat. It was up in the spring wires so I wouldn't notice it when I was cleaning the truck interior.

"Heavy shit Rob! I think you are going to need some professional help. Let's wait and see what we can find out from what we planted today. You need to be careful man. Anything you say or do in the house is being watched and listened to and everything you say in your truck is being recorded."

That night when Mandy got home from work I had dinner ready and on the table, but it was a quiet meal. All I had were questions I couldn't ask and I was actually afraid to open my mouth for fear of what might come out. I sat there thinking, "What the hell are you into Mandy? What the hell is going on?" Sitting and eating quietly is not the way I usually am and Mandy of course noticed it.

"Something wrong honey? You seem like your mind might be somewhere else."

"Just got the grave shift blues. I can't wait for the change to swings."

"I know what you mean lover. I need to get back to where you are cuddled up to me in bed at night."

"Only two more weeks."

"I have an idea lover. Why don't we let the dishes set and go on up to the bedroom for dessert? Then you can take a short nap before you have to go in to work."

"Lead the way."

I watched Mandy strip and marveled at the fact that I had managed to land a woman like her. She had been one hundred and ten pounds when I met her ten years before and she hadn't gained a pound. I never got tired of looking at her. She smiled as she looked at my erection and said:

"I see that you still seem to like what you see. The only thing is that it is so hard and I like my baby soft and cuddly. I guess I'll have to make the hardness go away."

She knelt in front of me, gave me a state of the art blow job and then pulled me onto the bed. I never did get to take the short nap and in fact I was almost late for work.

~~***~~

Work was a bitch that night. All I thought about were mini-cams, the tap on our telephone and the receiver in the attic and what they all meant. I wondered about what I would find when I got home. The receiver in the attic could only be checked when I wasn't at home and during grave turn I was around all the time except when I was at work. That meant that the only time it could be checked was after ten forty-five when I left for work and before I got home at eight. That meant that unless someone was sneaking into the house after Mandy left for work and before I got home the checker had to be Mandy - or someone Mandy let in after I was gone. Hal's theory was that if it was me being watched they would be checking the receiver almost every day.

The first thing I did when I got home was go up into the attic. The mini-cam that Hal had installed fed into a compact VCR that he had hidden under the attic insulation. I got the tape out of it, put a fresh one in, and then headed down into the basement. There was a spy cam watching my workshop area, but nothing in the rest of the basement so

Hal had rigged up a small TV, VCR and audio cassette player back behind the stored Christmas decorations.

I pushed the tape into the VCR and hit 'play'. There was about two seconds of black and then the screen showed the hatch into the attic being pushed up and moved to the side. The time stamp said 10:58 PM which was just a little time after I left for work. Then Mandy's head came up through the hatch. Until then, even though I knew it highly unlikely, I had hoped that whatever was going on that Mandy wasn't part of it. But there she was!

I watched as she walked over to the receiving unit and pushed buttons. She watched and listened to what was on the machine for about ten minutes and then left the attic. I checked the phone tap that Hal had put in. It was a voice activated cassette recorder and the counter read 217 so I popped out the tape and put a fresh one in and reset the counter. I was using headphones in case the spy cam in my workshop was sensitive enough to pick out other sounds in the basement so I put them on and rewound the tape and then hit the 'play' button. A man's voice said:

"Yes?"

"Good morning."

"Good morning to you. Everything normal at your end?"

"Everything seems normal. Nothing out of the ordinary."

"That's good. We don't need any complications. You know the plan for the day?"

"Of course."

"Just checking. Never hurts to check."

"It will get done. He reminded me last night so I need to make sure that you don't forget. He is off grave shift in two weeks and will be on afternoons for four months."

"That will of course be a big help and it can't happen soon enough."

"Have you figured out yet how you are going to work around it when he does his day shift turn?"

"No, not yet, but I'm sure that we will come up with something workable. Call me this afternoon."

"It won't be until after four."

"Doesn't matter; just be sure and call me and let me know how it went. Goodbye."

"Bye."

I sat there staring at the tape player and thinking, "What the hell is going on? What are you doing Mandy?"

~~***~~

Hal wasn't surprised when I told him that it was Mandy who checked on the receiver in the attic. Unlike me he wasn't in denial and he had known all along who it had to be. He listened to the phone conversation and shook his head.

"I said it already Rob, but this sounds bad. At the very least she is doing something that they do not want you to know about and it has got to be some heavy shit if they are using over thirty grand just to keep an eye on you. I think you need some professional help on this Rob."

"You said that once before. What do you mean by "professional" help?"

"I mean that you need a private detective to look into what Mandy is up to."

"I can't afford the kind of money that it would take to do something like that."

"Not necessarily true. You may be able to make it happen without money."

"How?"

"This guy I'm thinking of has a private plane. I think he said it was a Beechcraft Bonanza. Maybe you could work on his plane in exchange for him checking up on Mandy. He doesn't really need the money anyway. Being a private detective is more like a hobby with him."

"A hobby?"

"Yeah. He used to be a stockbroker or some other kind of financial whiz and he either made or came into a bunch of bucks and he retired and started a detective agency because he'd always had a fantasy about being a private eye. Turns out that he had a feel for it and has done well at it. But I would wait two weeks if I were you."

"Why?"

"Because you will be off midnights and on afternoons. Right now whatever she is doing has to be done during the day while she is at work, or supposed to be at work. When you go on swings she will have the evenings as well as the days to work with. It will give Glen a better shot at quickly finding out what is going on."

"I don't know if I can hold it in that long."

"Only you can be the judge of that. I'll call Glen today and ask him if he would be willing to do a deal with you."

"I'm going to get one of those prepaid cell phones today and not let Mandy know. I'll call you with the number when I get it. I don't want to use my regular cell. As high tech as all this stuff they are using is I don't want to gamble that my cell phone isn't bugged."

"Good thinking. I should have thought of that myself."

I called Hal at four and gave him the number of the pre-paid phone and he told me he had called his private eye friend and that the friend was interested in working out a deal and he gave me the man's name and phone number. I called Glen Hawthorne as soon as I disconnected from Hal and made an appointment to see him the next morning at eleven.

That evening I pretended that everything was fine and as far as I could tell Mandy accepted it. The next morning when I got home from work I didn't bother to check the attic cam since it had already shown me what I had needed to find out - who was checking the remote receiver - and I went right to the telephone tap.

"Good morning."

"Good morning. Everything okay?"

"He's been a little moody lately, but that isn't uncommon. He usually gets that way around the end of his grave shift turn."

"Did you get the message yesterday afternoon?"

"About being cancelled? Yes, I heard."

"Friday is still a go so check in with me tomorrow. Goodbye."

"Bye."

~~***~~

At eleven I walked in the door to the offices of the Hawthorne Investigative Agency and met Glen Hawthorne, owner and only employee. He already knew some of the story from Hal and I handed him the cassettes from the phone tap. He listened and raised an eye brow.

"They don't tell you anything that you can use, but they speak volumes as far as letting you know that something very sneaky is going on. Just what is it you want?"

"I want to know just what the hell is going on."

We struck a deal. He would do his detecting and I would do his one hundred hour and annual inspections on his Beechcraft until I had worked off his fee. In addition to the inspections I would do all the maintenance, but he would have to pay for the parts.

I gave him all the information on Mandy - her schedule (as I knew it) and where she worked, her cell number and the information on the car she drove. I told him about Hal's idea of waiting until I started on swing shift and he agreed that it was a good idea. He did want to do one thing as soon as possible though. He wanted a spy cam in my kitchen.

"That's where most people end up. They sit, talk, have coffee or a drink and they have a flat surface between them to write or draw on."

I made arrangements for him to have it done the next day.

I wasn't at all surprised when Hal showed up the next day to place the spy cam in the kitchen. He told me that he did all the electronic surveillance for Glen. I played that mornings tape for him. It was basically the same as the ones from the two previous days. A "Good morning" and an "Is everything okay on your end" and the information that nothing was scheduled for that day.

Mandy brought some work home with her that night so I went down into my basement workshop and worked on the bookcase I was making. In a way it was a relief because I didn't have to face her. If I didn't face her she wouldn't see that I was bothered by something. The last thing I needed right then was to make her worry and think she needed to be even more careful about what she was doing.

On Friday morning the man on the other end of the line said, "Have a nice weekend" and that told me that whatever Mandy was involved in was a Monday through Friday thing only. Trying to figure out what was going on was driving me nuts. Mandy's behavior towards me was the same as it had been since we started dating. She was loving, affectionate and our love life was great. We hadn't had an argument in years. I could not spot anything wrong in our relationship. What the hell could she be doing that she and whoever she was doing it with had to be so afraid of letting me find out? Well I'd start to maybe get some answers on Monday when I started working afternoons and Glen got to work on the problem.

I think I managed to get through the weekend without tipping Mandy off that all was not well. She didn't get a morning phone call because for the next four months I would be home in the mornings. She would either need to talk to the man on the phone in her office, on her cell or after I had gone to work. I made a mental note to ask Hal if we could put a voice activated tape recorder in her car like the one she had put into mine.

~~***~~

Tuesday morning after Mandy had left for work I reviewed the audio and video from Monday. There was nothing of interest on the video, but the audio tape had something.

"Hi. Just checking in. Is it still a go for tomorrow night?"

"As of two hours ago. I don't really expect that it will be cancelled. You sure that everything is cool on your end?"

"Should be no problems."

"There had better not be any problems. We are not paying you to have problems."

"And you won't have any!" Mandy snapped at him

They said their goodbyes, hung up and left me with something else to think about. Mandy was being paid? Did it have something to do with her job?

Wednesday morning at 8:13 is when my marriage ended. It turned out that we didn't need Glen to find out what Mandy was up to. Just the stuff that Hal planted in the house did the trick.

As soon as Mandy had left for work and I'd eaten breakfast I went to check the audio and video from Tuesday. The attic video showed Mandy downloading the receiver in what looked like a portable CD player. The camera in the living room captured Mandy coming into the room with a man I didn't recognize and they went over and sat on the couch. The man took Mandy in his arms and kissed her and then he asked her how much time he had. She told him that he needed to be gone by eleven and he said that he didn't think that would give him enough time. She giggled and said:

"You mean you still have something left after four hours in your hotel room?"

"I can never get enough of you and you know it."

"I just don't understand why you insist on making love to me here in my home and on my bed."

"Of course you do Mandy. You're mine and the best way to prove it is to have you here in your home, on your bed, your kitchen table, the washer and dryer, whatever."

"My husband just might have something to say about who I belong to."

"Fuck him! If he was strong enough to hold onto you I wouldn't be here."

"Would you like something to drink why I try and get you ready?"

"Scotch if you have it."

"Of course I have it sweetie. I knew you would be here so I made sure that I'd have your brand of scotch on hand."

"You knew I would be here?"

"Of course I did lover. I know what kind of man you are and I knew that sooner or later you would want me here. And don't give me any of that "I want you on your own bed" nonsense. You want me in my husband's house and on my husband's bed. You want to leave your smell in his house; take his wife in his own territory and don't you even try to deny it. Spread out and get comfy while I get you your scotch."

Mandy left the room and the man stood up, took off his trousers and briefs and then sat back down. He was stroking his cock when Mandy came back and handed him his drink. As he took a sip of his scotch Mandy went to her knees in front of him, leaned her head down and kissed the head of his cock. Then she licked the head and the shaft and took him in her mouth. She worked on him for several minutes and then he said:

"We need to take this to the bedroom baby."

"Your wish is my command lover."

Mandy got up and headed for the bedroom. By that time I had tears in my eyes. I loved that woman. Mandy had been my life from the day I first met her and I had spent the years following thinking that she felt the same about me. "Your wish is my command?" I was crushed. I forced myself to watch what took place in the bedroom. I was going to need some steel in my backbone for what was to come and the more I watched her betray me the harder that steel would become.

I watched as she lay back, smiled up at him and spread her legs wide. I listened as she moaned when he pushed his cock into her. I heard the cries and sounds that I thought I had been the only one to ever hear. I saw him finish, pull out and then move into a sixty-nine. I watched them lick and suck each other and then I watched him fuck Mandy a second time. I heard her tell him he had to leave.

"But why? He doesn't get off until eleven-thirty and he won't get home until after twelve. We have time."

"No we don't. I need to get these sheets off the bed and clean ones on and then I need to shower and douche before he gets home."

"Don't douche. I want to think of him feeling my cum on his dick."

"Oh sure, and what do I tell him when he asks why my pussy feels like a swamp? "Oh that? It's nothing. Just what my lover left in me." I don't think so."

"Just tell him that you are hot and wet because you got horny waiting for him to get home."

"You really want me to do that?"

"Absolutely!"

She was silent for a bit and then said, "Okay, but if it goes bad you may have to support me when he throws me out."

"You will do it?"

"Anything for you lover, you know that."

"If he catches on and splits you know my standing offer. I'll put you up in your own condo."

"That's sweet lover, but you do need to go, but be ready for my call if he doesn't like the feel of you."

I thought back to the previous night. Mandy met me when I came in the door. She was wearing a black lace nightgown, high heels and her make-up had been freshly done.

"I need you baby. I'm as horny as a goat and I need you. Come on baby, hurry to bed."

She hadn't felt any different from the other times I'd made love to her, but not knowing how long she had been fucking around on me I had no way of knowing that I wasn't the second man of the day every time we had gone to bed together. I remembered her comment about "four hours in your hotel room and I wondered how many times a week she met someone in a hotel room when she was supposed to be working. That prompted another thought. She was supposed to be at work so how did she get out of it? Did her boss know what she was doing? Was he involved somehow? All things that I would have to ask Glen to find out.

After watching the video I listened to the telephone tap.

"Hello?

"He's gone."

"Everything go okay?"

"He still wants to set me up as his mistress."

"Too bad we can't make it happen. It would sure make things better."

"Well it can't happen and if you know what is good for you you will make sure that it doesn't happen."

"I don't think that I like the tone of your voice."

"Tough shit! I know you and it would be just your style to let my husband find out so he would kick me out and I'd be free to be Sam's mistress."

"I would never do something like that."

"Yes you would and the only thing stopping you is the sure and certain knowledge that I would blow the whistle on you and every one of the half dozen or so men you have made me take care of. You destroy my marriage and I'll destroy you and don't you forget it!"

"I won't forget it. I'll see you tomorrow evening" and he hung up.

Now I had even more to think about. It sounded like Mandy was doing what she was doing under protest, but that meant nothing to me. The fact is that she was doing it and that is all that counted to me. The man she had taken care of the previous evening was bad enough, but by her own words there were also "a half dozen or so" others. How long had it been going on and why hadn't I ever gotten an inkling?

I called Glen and brought him up to date and told him to concentrate on the man Mandy had spent the afternoon with. He'd already known about the man since he had been on Mandy since I started swing shift. He told me that the man, Samuel Billings according to the hotel register, had taken Mandy to lunch and then back to his hotel room for a little over four hours and then he had followed them to my house. I told him that Mandy was going to see the man who was behind things that night and I told him that I wanted everything on Samuel Billings that he could get me. I intended to find out who the "half dozen or so" were, who it was who was having Mandy do what she was doing and then I was going to ruin them all.

~~***~~

Mandy was waiting up for me again when I got home that night. We had sex twice (not "made love" but had sex) before she cuddled up next to me and went to sleep. I lay there staring at the ceiling and thinking back over the last couple of years. There had been no change in Mandy's attitude toward me that I could see. She was affectionate and loving (or was a superb actress) and our sex life was as good as ever. I could not for the life of me point to something and say:

"There - right there! That's when whatever she is doing started."

When I finally fell asleep it was with a head full of questions that I had no answers for.

I waited an hour after Mandy left for work before I checked the audio and video. I gave her the hour in case she had forgotten something and came back to get it. There was nothing on the phone tap and the only video came from the camera that Glen had suggested we put in the kitchen and from the camera in our bedroom.

Mandy and a man walked into the kitchen and Mandy asked the man if he would like a drink and he said a beer would be fine if she had one. She got him a beer and herself a Diet Coke and then she sat down at the table with him.

"Do you have it?" he asked.

She took what looked like a CD from her pocket and slid it across the table to him. He opened his briefcase, took out an envelope and pushed it to her. She pushed it aside, leaned forward and said:

"Now what?"

"He's in town till Saturday. He has that dinner to go to tonight, but he wants to see you the rest of the nights he is here."

"Won't happen. Rob's days off while he is on swings are Friday and Saturday so those two nights are out."

"Couldn't you have a girl's night out with some friends or pretend to have an Avon party to go to?"

"I could, but I won't. I'm not giving up my time with Rob."

"It is only for this weekend. You will have all the rest for your husband."

"No John, I won't do it so leave it be."

It was a conversation that I could not get my head around. She is cheating on me, but won't give up our time together? It didn't make sense. He shrugged and got up and Mandy walked him to the door. After he left the bedroom camera showed Mandy going into her closet with the envelope she had been given and she came out without it. So, on my list of things to do as soon as I was done reviewing the audio and video was to take a look in Mandy's closet.

The closet in our bedroom is actually two closets. It runs the entire length of the long side of our 14 x 20 foot bedroom. Inside, at the mid-point, there is a wall that divides the closet into equal halves. One side is my walk-in closet and the other side is Mandy's. I usually have no need or reason to go into Mandy's half and in fact I couldn't remember the last time I was in there.

I started my search just inside the door and worked my way toward the back. I didn't find anything until I got to the very back. There were a dozen shoe and hat boxes and three medium sized moving boxes that had "Mother's things" written on the sides with a Magic Marker. Mandy's mother had passed away three years before and the boxes contained the things of her mom's that she just couldn't bear to part with. There wasn't anything in the shoe or hat boxes, but I hit pay-dirt when I opened the top box that said, "Mother's things."

There were eighteen CDs with names and dates written on them and fourteen envelopes like the one the John guy had pushed across the table to her the previous evening. I opened one and found it stuffed with hundreds, fifties and twenties. I counted it and found that the envelope had six thousand dollars in it. In the next box I found her douche bag and a collection of "come fuck me" high heels and lingerie that I had never seen her wear. I also found condoms, a diaphragm and a bottle of "morning after" pills. All good things for Mandy to have since I was sterile because of something that I'd had as a kid; mumps, chicken pox, diphtheria or something like that (and yes, I made sure that Mandy knew before we got married). The third box did have her mother's things in it.

I went and got a pen and a piece of paper and wrote down the names that were on the CDs and then I went and called Glen and gave him what I had. When I hung up from talking to Glen I went back to Mandy's closet and counted the money in the envelopes. The largest amount was twelve thousand and the smallest was three thousand. The total was seventy-four thousand dollars. I made a note of the brand of CDs and then I took three of them and went downstairs and put them in the CD player. It was pretty much the same as what she had done with Billings. She sucked and fucked all three men several times before telling them that they needed to leave before I got home.

I took the three back upstairs and put everything back the way I'd found it. I'd never lifted a hand to woman in my life, but had Mandy walked in just then I couldn't swear that I wouldn't have hurt her.

I managed to get myself under control and by the time I left for work I had the rough outline of a plan in my mind. To make it work meant that I would have to control myself and pretend that everything was fine. I could not do anything that would make Mandy suspect that I was in the least bit suspicious. The problem was that I didn't know if I could do it.

~~***~~

She wasn't at the door when I came home that night, but she did wake up and reach for my cock when I got in bed. I told her I was too weary to have sex and she told me not to worry, that she would do all the work. She slid down, took me in her mouth and sucked me off. Sometimes she swallowed and sometimes she didn't, but that night she did and then she moved up, snuggled in against me, whispered "I love you" and went back to sleep.

I lay there, staring up at the ceiling, and trying to make it all add up. Everything she said to me and did to me was what a loving wife would do and say, but how could she when she was doing what she was doing? It just did not equate!

The next day's audio was the John guy calling to make sure that everything was a go for the evening and then a call from Mandy to John telling him that Billings had just left and that everything had gone well. The video was almost a rerun of the last time; a starter hum job on the couch, a move to the bedroom, a fuck followed by a sixty-nine, another fuck and then a suck job in an attempt to get him up one more time (which failed and that pleased me no end) and then she saw him out. She showered, made the bed and then got in bed and starting reading a book and at that point I stopped watching.

There was an interesting bit of dialog that took place. She spread her legs and waited for him and while he undressed he said:

"Tell me again."

"Tell you what?"

"You know damned well what baby."

"Does it make you especially hard to know that my husband soaked his cock in your cum?"

"You'll see just how hard in a few seconds."

"He pushed his cock in my pussy and it just slid all the way in with no resistance at all. I didn't give him a chance to ask me why I was so wet. I moaned and said, "Oh God baby, I'm so horny. I've been thinking of this all day. I told him that I had been so hot thinking about fucking him that I'd gone to the bathroom twice to get myself off and even that wasn't enough. I told him I used my hairbrush when I got home." She giggled and said, "I threw in the hairbrush in case he got to thinking about how loose I was.

"You fucking slut" he moaned as he got on the bed.

"There is one thing that I didn't tell you earlier in your hotel room. He wanted to eat me before he fucked me, but I didn't dare let him. He isn't stupid. He's eaten me hundreds of times and he knows my taste. He would have noticed the difference. Does that turn you on lover? Does knowing that I really wanted to let him taste you make you excited?"

By then he was pushing his cock into her and her legs had come up to clamp him. "You would like that wouldn't you? You love the thought of my husband slurping up your juices don't you?"

"You slut!" he cried as he drove himself into her and she laughed and moaned. "Fuck me lover, fuck me hard."

~~***~~

It was my first day off so I was home when Mandy got home from work. I had dinner ready and she told me that she wanted to take a quick shower before eating.

"I was in a smoke filled conference room most of the day and I've got it in my hair and on my clothes and I stink!"

That told me that she probably spent part of the afternoon with Billings or some other guy and needed to wash the smell of him off of her before I noticed. Probably wanted to flush some of him out of her while she was at it. That thought brought out a bit of the mean streak in me and I started up to the bathroom shedding clothes as I went. She was already in the shower with the water running when I got there. Her panties were lying on the floor and I glanced down at them and saw that the crotch was soaked.

Her back was to me and her legs were spread wide as she worked on her cunt with a rag. She apparently didn't hear me push the shower curtain aside, get in and slide the curtain closed. The first she knew I was there was when I grabbed her hips, leaned forward so my knees would keep her legs from closing and then I pushed my cock at her pussy. By pure luck my aim was good and the head of my cock entered her and then one good push and I slid in as far as I could go. She was slick and slippery and Billings was getting his wish -- my cock was soaking in his juices (at least I assumed it was Billings). I remembered what she had told Billings, that I had "slid in with no resistance at all" and I wondered if she remembered that conversation as I slid so easily into her.

Once I was fucking her, Mandy leaned forward, put her hands against the wall and spread her legs even farther apart. She started moaning and crying out and I wondered if she was thinking of what kind of story she could tell me to cover how slippery her cunt was.

I fucked her hard and steady until I came and then I pulled out and told her to hand me the wash rag.

"I'll do your back for you while I'm here."

While I scrubbed her back I wondered if that was the first time I'd slid my cock into someone else's soup or if she had douched every time before coming to me. We finished showering together and then I told her I was going to wash my hair while I was in the shower (I noticed that she hadn't washed hers which was why she was going to shower in the first place -- to get the cigarette smoke out of her hair -- and I wondered if she would realize that at some point during the evening).

My real reason for letting her get out first was to give her a chance to hide her panties and sure enough when I got out of the shower they were gone. I also wondered if she was getting so used to cheating that she was getting sloppy in her actions. Why hadn't she showered and cleaned up in Billings' hotel room? If she knew she was going to meet him why not a spare pair of clean panties in her purse? Why take a chance coming home freshly fucked when she knew I'd be home when she got there? Granted, I rarely jumped her bones when she first got home, but I did it occasionally so why take the chance?"

Over dinner Mandy asked, "What got into you tonight?"

"I thought you might like it. You were ready last night and I didn't take care of you."

"Yes you did. You held me and snuggled with me and I needed that."

"Still, you got me off and I didn't reciprocate."

"You know I like taking you in my mouth and making you feel good. There shouldn't be any "you have to do me because I do you." I love you baby, and I like to make you feel good."

I made no mention of how slick and slippery she was when I fucked her in the shower and not surprisingly, she didn't mention it either.

We made it through my days off without me letting anything show that I was onto her. For her part she was as attentive and loving as always. Once, when she thought I was napping on the couch she came over, bent down and kissed me lightly on the forehead, whispered "I love you" and then went out into the kitchen. I didn't doubt that she meant it because she thought I was asleep so she wouldn't have been putting on an act, but how could she love me and do what she was doing? It didn't matter how often I looked at it or from what angle, it still did not compute.

Twice I almost brought it out into the open, but both times I stopped because it would mean my giving up on my plan to find out about all the men she had been seeing and getting even. Taking my revenge was paramount and if Mandy knew that I knew she would no doubt let the John guy know and I would lose the element of surprise. I did not want them to see it coming.

~~***~~

The only video Monday was of Mandy checking the receiver before she went to bed, but there was audio from the phone tap.

"Hello?"

"It's me."

"You have anything for me?"

"Just what happened here Thursday evening."

"I'll pick it up Monday. Meet me for lunch at Augustino's and you can give it to me then. Are you ready for Wednesday?"

"As I'll ever be."

"You don't sound enthused sweetie."

"Am I supposed to?"

"I certainly hope you show your dates more enthusiasm than I'm hearing right now."

"Have you had any complaints so far?"

"No, and I don't want to get any."

"I'm tired. I'm going to bed" and she hung up on him.

I called Glen and gave him the information that Mandy would be doing something on Wednesday and he gave me the run down on what he had found out about Samuel Billings. Thirty-eight years old, married to Carol for fifteen years and the father of Ralph (13) and Kathy (10). He was Chief Procurement Officer for Apollo Industries, a company that made something fairly secret for the U.S. Department of Defense.

Glen had been outside my house waiting when John left following his meeting with Mandy and he had followed John. He was still digging, but he was able to tell me that John's full name was John David Gaynor and that he was the Vice President of Sales and Marketing for the Maxxim Corporation, a company that was heavy into engineering and manufacturing. Glen hoped to have more for me in a couple of days. I mentioned that it appeared that Gaynor was collecting stuff he could use to blackmail or coerce the men Mandy was fucking and that the other names I'd given him probably had something to do with buying from or selling to Maxxim and that could possibly be a starting point in finding out who they were.

Wednesday and again on Thursday Mandy entertained a man in our bedroom. She called him Frank and there was a Frank Stemper written on one of her hidden CDs. It was more suck and fuck and wasn't anything different than what she had done with Billings.

I reviewed the tapes every morning and most of what I got out of it was Gaynor calling to make sure everything went all right the night before and arranging to meet Mandy for lunch so she could give him what the receiver recorded. On Friday morning the phone tap gave me something that I gave to Glen. It was the usual stuff up to the point where Gaynor said:

"Is Sunday set?"

"Yes. I'll leave to meet him as soon as my husband goes to work."

My days off passed quickly and on Monday morning Glen told me that Mandy had left the house fifteen minutes after I had left for work and had driven to the Motel 6 on Ferguson. She had knocked on the door of room 118, the door had opened and she had stepped inside. A small bribe had gotten him the information that the room was registered to a Rhett Baxter. Baxter was also one of the names on Mandy's secret tapes. Mandy was in room 118 until eleven o'clock at which time she left the room and drove home.

I discovered that I was not the patient man I'd always thought I was. My original intent was to find out who all seven of the men were who had been fucking Mandy and then find a way to get payback, but at the end of four weeks I only had Gaynor, Stemper, Billings and Baxter. I was sick of listening to audio and watching video of my wife betraying me and I wanted it over. I decided that it was time to end it.

I saw an attorney and got the paper work for the divorce moving. I used my computer to burn copies of Mandy's secret CDs and then waited until my attorney told me that everything was in place. On Thursday, May 5th at eleven-ten a man approached Mandy at her place of work and asked her if she was Amanda Haight and when she said yes he handed her an envelope and said:

"You have been served."

When Mandy opened her envelope she found that in addition to being sued for divorce on the grounds of infidelity she was also under a restraining order keeping her at least 500 feet from me and the house. The only way she would be allowed in the house was if she arranged for a court supervised visit to pick up her things. I also enclosed a note telling her she could call and leave a message on the answering machine telling me what she would like to have placed in garbage bags and set out 500 feet from the house. I also told her not to bother trying to call me on the home phone or my cell as I had absolutely no interest in talking to her. That was a lie of course. I wanted to know just what the hell had been going on, but I wanted her to sweat for a while before we sat down to talk.

At the same time that Mandy was being served, give or take five minutes, Gaynor, Billings, Baxter and Stemper were being served papers informing them that they were being sued for Alienation of Affections. Also at the same time special messengers were delivering packages to the wives of Gaynor, Billings, Stemper and the fiancée of Baxter.

The morning all the paperwork was being served was a busy one for me. I had given Hal and Glen all the surveillance gear that Mandy and Gaynor had placed in the house and they were busy removing it. A locksmith was there changing all the locks on the house and the man from Terminex was there spreading ant bait around the perimeter of the house. And of course Mandy ignored my note and my cell started beeping every four or five minutes and between those calls the house phone rang and I heard the answering machine pick up.

"Rob? Are you there? Rob? Pick up the phone Rob. Come on Rob; we need to talk."

I ignored both phones.

Even though Hal and Glen had removed all of the devices that Mandy and Gaynor had put in the house I had them leave what they had put in. I ignored Mandy's attempts to get in touch with me and waited for what I knew would happen next. I knew Mandy would ignore the restraining order just as she had ignored my note telling her not to bother calling me.

Sure enough, when I came home from work Sunday night and checked the video tapes the kitchen camera showed Mandy coming into the kitchen through the door that led to the basement. The bedroom camera showed her going into her closet and then coming out with a look on her face that could kill. Probably upset that her CDs and her seventy-four thousand dollars weren't there. The attic camera showed her sticking her head up through the hatch and seeing that the Hallman XK116 digital recorder was gone. I walked down to the basement and saw that one of the windows was broken out and I called the police and reported the break in. I gave them copies of the tapes from my "security system" and told them I was missing three credit cards, one thousand dollars in cash and my Smith and Wesson .38 Special. Lies of course, but I wanted to make things as difficult for Mandy as I could.

I casually commented on the fact that I couldn't understand why she took the revolver and then I suddenly said, "Oh shit!" and one of the detectives asked "What?"

"She isn't all that happy about our divorce. You don't think that she…? No, she wouldn't. At least I don't think she would. You think maybe I should buy a bulletproof vest?"

I told them where she worked and at nine in the morning they arrested her while her fellow employees looked on. She was charged with breaking and entering, theft and as a separate count of theft - theft of a firearm - and violation of a restraining order. Her father put up her bail and when I got home from work that night there was a message from Mandy on the answering machine. Short and to the point, "You bastard!" I smiled as I deleted it.

~~***~~

I had intended to take what I had and go see the President and CEO of Maxxim and ask him if he was aware of Gaynor's activities, but then decided not to. I was suing Gaynor and costing him his job would mean a loss of income for him so I decided to wait until the suit was settled before doing that.

I was getting two and three phone calls a day from Mandy, but I didn't take any of them. She sent me letters and I returned them to her unopened. She sat on the hood of my car in the parking lot at the hanger and waited for me to get off so I took the employee bus over to the terminal and took a taxi home from there.

Over the next month I heard from everyone on both sides of the family telling me that I wasn't being fair in not talking to Mandy and I told them all the same thing. She had cheated on me with seven different men, had gotten caught and we had nothing to talk about. By cheating on me she had forfeited any right to be able to communicate with me. I would sit down with her and let her talk, but it would be at a time of my choosing, not hers.

Quite frankly, I wanted her to suffer. The fact that I was suffering too didn't much matter to me. The problem was that I loved her. Even knowing what she had done I loved her. The problem was compounded by the fact that I really believed that she loved me. What I could not get my head around was how could she love me and do what she had done? Going by the hidden CDs she'd had been sexually intimate with AT LEAST seven different men over the last year and a half. Men she fucked and then came home to me with their stink still on her. Oh I know she probably showered before she came to me, but their hands had been on her and their cocks had been in her and showering couldn't remove that. She had to be thinking of those hands and those cocks as she snuggled up next to me even if it was only to think that she was glad to be snuggling with me instead of lying under them. They HAD to be on her mind when she was with me.

~~***~~

I did not travel in the same social or business circles as Gaynor, Billings, Baxter or Stemper so I had no idea how they were fairing as far as wives and fiancées were concerned, but my lawyer informed me that their lawyers had been in contact with him. Gaynor and Baxter were denying everything and said they would go to court and take their chances. Billings and Stemper offered to settle out of court and I told my attorney to go ahead and settle. I didn't want a prolonged court fight; I just wanted to hurt the bastards.

I sent a note to Baxter and told him that while I had seen to it that his wife knew what he'd been doing with mine I had not yet shared that information with his employer, but that could change at any time. Two days later he offered to settle. That left Gaynor. He was the man who had pulled the strings. Mandy's pimp as it were, and he was the one I really wanted to hurt. But all I had on him was some taped conversations and the video of him sitting at our kitchen table passing Mandy an envelope and receiving a disc from her. To get him I was going to need a lot more and there was only one place I could get it.

The next time that Mandy called I took the call.

"Hello?"

"Rob, it's Mandy."

"Yes?"

"How are you?"

"I've been better, but not recently."

"I'd like to talk to you Rob."

"About what?"

"About the mess we are in."

"What mess would that be Amanda? I've separated myself from the mess you made of my life."

"Please Rob, I love you. I need to explain what was happening. It wasn't what you think it was. Please Rob; please let me talk to you."

I gave her about five seconds of silence and then said, "All right Amanda. The house at seven tonight, but I will have some questions and I had better get honest answers. The first time I even think you are not being honest with me you are out the door and there will not be a next time. You get one shot and tonight is it. Do you understand?"

"Yes. I won't lie to you Rob, I promise."

"Would that be anything like the promise you made me when we got married? You know, the one where you promised to be faithful to me?"

"I'm sorry Rob. I guess I deserved that, but there will be no untruths. I'll see you tonight. Goodbye."

She was parked out in front of the house at twenty to seven. I don't know if she sat there trying to work up the courage to face me or if she felt that since I said seven she had better follow my instructions to the "T" and didn't want to be even a minute late. What I do know is that watching her walk up to the house hurt. She was as beautiful as ever and it killed me to be apart from her.

She rang the doorbell at seven exactly and I let her in and told her we would use the kitchen. When we got there I pointed at a chair and said:

"You sit there and I'll sit over here where Gaynor sat when you gave him the recording and he gave you the envelope full of money."

I saw the look on her face when I said that and I said, "You weren't the only one with hidden cameras in the house. That should tell you that I know a whole lot more than you think I do. I do have a way to know if you try to sneak a lie by me."

"I told you Rob, no untruths and I meant it."

I placed a tape recorder on the table in front of me and hit the record button and said, "Okay Amanda, you called this meeting."

She looked at me and was silent for a moment and then said, "I need you to know one thing Rob, I need you to know that I love you. I love you with all my heart and soul and I would give anything if I could just go back in time and change some things. I do love you Rob and nothing that happened was because of anything you did or didn't do. I didn't do what I did because I stopped loving you; I did it because I love you so much that I couldn't bear the thought of losing you."

I just sat there and listened as I silently looked at her."

"What I did Rob, I did because I was blackmailed into doing it."

She saw I was getting ready to open my mouth and she held up a hand and said:

Please let me get it out Rob. This is the hardest thing I've ever had to do, so please let me get it all out before you say anything. When I'm done I'll answer any questions that you have, but please let me get it all out first."

She looked at me for a second and then asked, "Could I have a glass of wine? It will help steady my nerves. I opened a bottle of white wine and set it and a glass down in front of her and then sat down and waited. She poured some wine in her glass, took a sip and then told me the story.

It had happened during my swing shift turn almost two years ago. The company she was working for had a cocktail party for their clients and since I was working, Mandy's boss asked her if she would act as hostess. Since I wouldn't be home until after mid-night Mandy said she would do it. In addition to one of the large halls at the Hyatt Regency her company had also arranged for a hospitality suite. The first couple of hours went by without incident and then Mandy had started feeling funny. She felt a little disoriented and woozy and her boss told her to go on up to the hospitality suite and lie down. She didn't remember the next part, but she knew it had happened because she was shown the video.

Phil, her boss, had gone up to check on her and when he bent down to ask if she was all right she had grabbed his tie and pulled him down on the bed. She had rolled on top of him and kissed him and then she had unzipped his fly and had gone down on him.

I knew Phil and I liked him. I knew him well enough to know that he would never hit on Mandy, but I also knew that he wouldn't fight her off if she was the aggressor. Anyway, she sucked his cock, pulled his pants off and mounted him. He came, she sucked him hard and he fucked her again. She tried to go down on him and get him up a third time, but he pushed her away and said he needed to see to his guests. Phil was no sooner out the door than Baxter came in and after Baxter there were three men she didn't know. By the time Baxter was doing her for the second time she was becoming aware of what was happening, but she couldn't stop it and by the time the other three came back for seconds she was an eager participant.

"That was the night Phil called you and told you that the company put me up in a room because they felt I'd had too much to drink."

Baxter and the three men had taken turns on her until about two in the morning and then they left. The next morning, Amanda woke up with a hurting head, a very sore pussy and her body ached all over. She cleaned herself up and went into work.

She hadn't seen the video yet so she didn't know about Phil and she had wondered why he had avoided her all day. She did know that she had been fucked by four men who she didn't know and when she came home from work that night she was determined to tell me what had happened, but as soon as she saw me she lost her nerve.

She had gone into work the next morning determined to build up the courage to face me when she got home that night, but at eleven-thirty Phil had called her into his office and John Gaynor was there. She knew that Gaynor did a lot of business with the company, but she didn't realize how important he was until Phil said:

"John needs to talk with you about something. Why don't you take a long lunch."

She couldn't figure out what Gaynor wanted to talk with her about, but it all became clear when they got to the restaurant. He slid a half dozen photographs across the table to her and casually asked her what I might think if I was to receive copies or maybe even get a copy of the video.

"I could not let you see those pictures and if there was a video it could only be ten times worse than the pictures. Even to me it looked like I was loving it and I KNEW that I hadn't done it on purpose."

She found out later that Baxter had commented to Gaynor that he would love to fuck Mandy and Gaynor had asked what it would be worth to be able to do it. Baxter had said that for something as nice as Mandy he would give all of his business to Maxxim instead of just a portion. Gaynor had said, "Deal!"

Gaynor had slipped Mandy a "date rape cocktail," apparently it was something that he did often and he always had some in his car, his briefcase or his pocket. When Phil told Mandy to go up to the hospitality suite Gaynor said he was on his way up to his room and he offered to walk Mandy the room and make sure that she got there okay.

He got Mandy on the bed and then hurried up to room he had already rented. He had planned on setting up a buyer from another company with a hooker and taping it. He hurried to the room, got the camera and took it back to the hospitality suite. He hid the camera, turned it on and went to get Baxter. By the time he got back to the room Mandy and Phil were already at it.

The deal was simple. Gaynor needed a favor and if Mandy would do it he would give her the photos and the video. The favor was an afternoon with one of his customers. She had, just had, to get those pictures and the video that went with them and given what she had already been through what was one more? One more and she would be out from under the hammer. She would still tell me what happened, but she would tone it down some - like maybe confine it to Baxter - but the big thing was that I would never see the pictures and the video.

She agreed to do the one time favor, spent the afternoon in a hotel room with his customer and Gaynor gave her the photos and the video from the cocktail party. She destroyed them and then started to work up the courage to face me and tell me about the cocktail party and what had happened. I had worked overtime that night so her confession was going to have to wait until the next day.

The next day, Gaynor called her and told her that he needed another favor. He had another customer who needed to be taken care of. She had laughed at him and told him no way and to forget it. He had no hold over her now that she had the photos and video. Then Gaynor told her that yes, she did have the originals, but he had copies and he also had the tape that he had made of her when she took care of his customer the previous afternoon.

From then on she had been Gaynor's whore. To forestall any attempt she might later make against him by going to the authorities over his blackmailing her he started paying her a commission on sales that happened after she took care of one of his 'friends' and he did it in his rented apartment so he had her on tape taking the money and putting it in her purse.

The setup in our house had a dual purpose. One, to tape her meetings at the house and two, Gaynor wanted to keep an eye on me to see if I ever got suspicious and started checking up on Mandy. He had a good thing going with her, especially with guys like Baxter and Billings who kept coming back for more, and he didn't want to lose it so he kept an eye on me so he could adapt if I began to suspect something.

Mandy finally woke up to the fact that if he could use the tapes against her she could use them against him and she started making two copies of everything she took off of the receiving unit. She kept one set for herself and when the time came she was going to tell Gaynor "no more" and when he threatened her with showing me the tapes she would tell him if he did she would blow the whistle on him to every guy he'd had her do.

"And when was that going to happen?"

"As soon as I had a hundred thousand dollars. I was going to tell you what I had done and I wanted to have enough money to fall back on if you threw me out."

"If I threw you out? You thought that maybe I wouldn't?"

"I had hopes that you might love me as much as I love you and you would understand why I did what I did. I didn't want to lose you Rob and I couldn't see any way that I wouldn't if you ever saw that video tape. I had no choice Rob. I didn't dare gamble that you would stay with me after seeing the video. I was uncertain over the outcome if I just confessed to the cocktail party, but without the video I thought I might just have a chance. There was no chance at all if you had seen me with Baxter and those others."

"How many times did you have to do Phil to get him to give you all that time off to go play in hotels?"

"The only time I did anything with Phil was the night of the party. He let me have time off, with pay, anytime Gaynor said he needed me. He didn't really want to, but Gaynor had shown him pictures of Phil and me doing it and had hinted that it would sure be a shame if Phil's wife were to get a set."

"I suppose Phil will let you go now that I've blown the whistle on everyone."

"No. Phil and I have talked about things and we are both holding our breath to see what Gaynor might do. He can't hurt me anymore and he has no reason to hurt Phil, but who can tell? Phil knows I wasn't myself that night so we have been able to get back to a good relationship."

"Is that it? Anything else before you leave?"

She hesitated for a few seconds and then said, "I was hoping that I could convince you to give me the money that you took from my closet. Now that you have kicked me out I could use it."

"Sorry, but you are just going to have to consider that as the price you paid for stabbing me in the back. I might consider giving you some of it if you agree to testify against him if I end up taking him to court."

"Of course I will and I'll do it for nothing."

"I'll let you know" and I stood up to signal that as far as I was concerned her visit was over.

She looked up at me.

"Is there no chance Rob? Isn't there any chance at all that we can work through this and stay together? I love you, Rob. God knows that I do."

"I can't see how Amanda. There might have been a chance if you had told me about the cocktail party right after it happened, but now, all these months and all these men later? I don't see how."

She had tears in her eyes as I walked her to the door and there were tears in mine as I watched her drive away.

~~***~~

The next day, I went to Maxxim's in-town office complex and made my way to Gaynor's office. I walked right past his secretary who jumped up and told me that I couldn't go in. I smiled at her and said:

"It's okay sweetie, he is expecting me."

He was sitting at his desk and reading some papers when I walked in. He looked up and I saw recognition register on his face.

"Mr. Gaynor I believe" I said, "I'm Mandy's husband, but I expect that you already know that."

He started to stand up and I said, "No need to get up, I won't be here that long."

I dropped an envelope on his desk and said, "You weren't the only one with hidden cameras in my house. You will find four things in that envelope. One is a copy of the video of you giving my about to be ex-wife an envelope full of money in exchange for a recording of her evening with Billings. The second item is a copy of that evening with Billings. That's just there to let you know that Amanda made herself a copy of everything that you had her do in our house so your hidden cameras could record it. Item number three is excerpts from a tape that Amanda made for me last night and those excerpts will let you know she has agreed to testify against you if things end up in court which is exactly where things will end up if you do not make use of the fourth item which is a card with my attorney's phone number on it. I would strongly suggest that you call him and let him know that you are going to settle the lawsuit I have against you. If you do not make that call I will drop everything that I have on the District Attorney's desk this coming Friday."

I turned to leave the office and when I reached the door I turned back to him and said, "Hey; you have a fine day now" and then I left.

The next day, I got a call from my attorney telling me that Gaynor had called him and agreed to settle out of court. I waited until all the checks had cleared and the dust had settled and then I made six copies of everything I had and sent one set to the president and CEO of Maxxim and one copy each to the five man board of directors. Three days later, I got a phone call from a very pissed off (and, as it turned out, a recently unemployed) John Gaynor.

"You mother fucking bastard! You said if I settled you wouldn't do anything."

"No, that is not what I said. I said if you settled I would not give it to the District Attorney so he could file criminal charges against you. I didn't say anything about not telling your boss. And just so you know; it is all about revenge. You fucked me and I got even."

I hung up the phone and Mandy asked, "Who was that?"

"Your ex-pimp. He is upset because somehow his boss found out what he was doing and it upset him so much that he fired Gaynor."

~~***~~

Yes, Mandy is back in the house. Not back in my good graces, but back in the house. She is sleeping in the spare bedroom until we can see if we can put things back together. I'm not at all sure that we can. I do love her and I do believe she loves me so I'm willing to give it a try, but I don't know if that love will be enough. There are issues that have to be addressed, trust being one of them.

One of the others is that Mandy was right when she said she thought we might have a chance as long as I never saw the video of her taken at that cocktail party. I never did see that video, but I watched every one of the other videos that she had hidden in her closet and the images of Mandy with those other men are burned into my brain and every time I look at Mandy they start playing in my head.

I told her I would try and I will. I will try really hard. But I'm not making any promises.

The End

Here is a preview of another story you may enjoy:

THE
PRODIGAL
Family
THE ABBOTTS

It had been one hell of an eighteen-month roller coaster ride. I was living in my own soap opera. Me? I'm Robert Courtney Abbott. A forty-eight-year-old successful business man, married for twenty six years to Beverly Abigail Abbott, nee Sterns and with two children: Robert Courtney Abbott, Junior (affectionately called Deuce) and Stephanie Anne Abbott.

My wife Beverly is a vice president at a large advertising agency and it is that agency that I blame in large part for the current situation. Well, it is easier than taking the blame myself and besides, it is so much more comforting to put the blame elsewhere.

The Abbotts are a tad more than "slightly" well off, but I do so dislike the term "rich" so I settle for saying that we are "comfortable." Bev does not need to work, but she informed me early on that she intended to have a career and laid out my choices - a career-oriented Beverly or no Beverly at all. I do have to admit that if I knew back then that her career would put me in the situation that I now find myself in, I would still have chosen Beverly.

The Abbotts are health Nazis. We eat right, exercise religiously and as a result the four of us are in fine physical form, Beverly at forty-seven looks every bit of thirty-four and it pleases me that most people think that I'm not a day over thirty-six when in fact my half century mark is fast approaching.

Deuce is a recent college graduate with a degree in Electrical Engineering and he has chosen to go off and do his own thing rather than join the family business as I had hoped. I am disappointed, but it is his life so it gets to be his choice. Deuce lettered in every sport he put his hand to in high school, including some that I'd never even heard of, and still maintained an A average. He was offered athletic scholarships to a dozen well-known colleges and universities, but he turned them all down. He said he had enjoyed his childhood, but that it was now time to grow up and prepare for his future as a man and he buckled down and went to work on a degree in Electrical Engineering at the college close to home.

Stephanie Anne is in her final year at Smith and I believe that she is majoring in Economics, but I can't really be sure since she has changed majors so often. Deuce says that the only major that Steph really pursues is popularity. I think the boy is a tad jealous. Steph has been surrounded by swains since she was thirteen. She is drop dead gorgeous just like her mother, a straight A student and she lettered in track in high school and plays soccer and field hockey now that she is in college.

All of the above to offer just the briefest of glimpses of the Abbotts and now to the current situation that I find myself in.

~~***~~

We need to go back eighteen months to set the stage. We own a summer house on the lake and every August we go there for a three-week vacation. That particular August there were four of us at the summer house. Stephanie Anne was off backpacking in Europe with some friends. Deuce had brought along his fiancée Amber and then there was Bev and me.

Amber was a gorgeous young creature and an absolute joy to the eyes when she wore her bikinis - especially her "wicked weasels" - and my ribs were still sore a month later from all the elbows that Bev kept jabbing in my ribs whenever she caught me looking at Amber. Of course, Bev looked just as fantastic in her bikini so between Bev and Amber I was in an almost constant state of erection and I was more than happy to share those erections with my lovely wife.

Two weeks went by and then one Tuesday Bev received a phone call from her agency. There was a major problem with one of their largest and most important accounts and they needed her to return to work as soon as possible. Forty-five minutes later she was gone and there I was with no one to share my Amber-generated erections with.

Wednesday, Deuce and Amber hooked up with some kids on the other side of the lake and went to a party. I spent part of the day out on the lake fishing and the rest of it lounging around. I went to bed around ten with a book and half an hour later I was asleep.

According to the bedside clock it was two-thirty in the morning when the hot mouth on my cock woke me up. That was one of Bev's favorite tricks when she was horny and I was asleep. She would wake me with a blow job and once I was stiff enough to suit her she would attempt to turn me into a ruined wreck. Obviously she had just gotten back from the city and was horny. Once I was awake I grabbed her and maneuvered her over me in a sixty-nine and went to work on her pussy. She moaned as my tongue delved into her and she pushed her pussy down at me. I munched on her muffin and she moaned around my cock in her mouth. I worked on her pussy for several minutes and was surprised when she had an orgasm. Bev rarely has an orgasm when I eat her so I guessed she must have been super horny.

She was still shaking from her climax when I moved behind her and eased my cock into her. Bev shoved back at me which told me that she wanted me to go fast and hard so I gripped her hips with both hands and drove into her. Because of the time she had spent on my cock I was only able to go five or six minutes, but it was long enough for me to bring her off once more. I pulled out and fell to the bed next to her and put my arms around her, expecting some snuggle time, but she pulled away from me, swung around and went for my cock again. She moved over me in a sixty-nine and it dawned on me what was happening.

It wasn't the first time that it had happened and when it did it made her extremely horny. Bev was a hot-looking babe and she got hit on a lot. Every once in a while a really hot guy would make a determined run at her and while she deflected the pass, it nonetheless made her horny as hell. While she was in the city, someone must have made a move on her.

I dug into her pussy and worked on it and damn if I didn't give her another orgasm. By then I was stiff again so I fucked her for about ten minutes giving her two more orgasms before I had mine. This time when I pulled her to me she moved in tight and we fell asleep.

Daylight was coming in through the window and I was in that half-awake-half-asleep state when I heard "Oh shit!" I opened my eyes and saw not Bev but Amber. She was looking at me wide-eyed…

If you enjoyed this sample then look for **The Prodigal Family: The Abbotts.**

Here's another preview of a book you may also enjoy:

Suspicion

BOOK 1

ELUSIVE BILLIONAIRE ROMANCE SERIES

SHYLA STARR

"I want to know who the hell is responsible for this mess!" boomed Hendrick from the front of the boardroom.

Silence filled the room as all the top people in the company stared at Hendrick in awe. They knew he wasn't the kind of guy to be messed with. Considering the company had just been charged with federal and criminal charges for dumping industrial waste into the Arctic Ocean, they knew it was best to stay silent.

"I return from vacation to find the prosecutor in my office to tell me that a company that I built from the ground up to help humanity is being accused of filling the ocean with waste! Waste??" He screamed across the table, his face turning an angry red. Hendrick stopped for a moment to compose himself and looked at each person at the table, assessing their worth.

"Pray it was not one of you frontrunners that made the decision to handle the waste of the company in this manner. Now go, and I expect reports hourly about how we are making this right and where waste should be going from now on."

Everyone got up from the table quickly and filtered out of the room. Hendrick watched them all leave and turned to his right-hand man, Geoffrey, the CEO of the company.

"Tell me you didn't know."

A broad-shouldered man, Geoffrey held an imposing frame that fit well with the red beard that made him appear like a Viking. He was incredibly loyal and a great asset to the company.

"You have known me your whole life, Hendrick. I'm sure you know I had nothing to do with dumping waste into the ocean. The person in charge of a decision like that is one of your minions."

"How is it that the owner and CEO of a company had no idea that his own company has been poisoning the ocean?"

"Someone down the line obviously felt it would save the company a lot of money."

Hendrick snorted, "Ya and no one would ever find out that the Arctic Ocean was suddenly polluted? My god, they have vessel numbers and everything, it was our guys to be sure, so how do I not know about it?"

"The prosecutors are doing their investigation and so are we. I can guarantee that we will find out who is responsible before anyone else does."

"I'm being prosecuted, Geoffrey! They think I knew about this madness."

"Look, you didn't know and they can't prove that you did. You will have your day in court and they will simply have to let it go. They can't pull evidence from thin air so you're safe."

Hendrick went to the side table by the grand picture window. He poured them both a glass of bourbon, handing one to Geoffrey.

"I built this company because I believed in a vision and now our reputation is being smeared. All the while I'm off doing fundraisers and charity events while some asshole is destroying the ocean under my name."

"Hendrick, it's your job to do those things. That's how money is raised and you don't need to be at the company all the time. That's my job, to handle the bullshit. I apologize that this issue slipped through my fingers. I assure you it will be handled. We certainly won't be dealing with such an issue as this in the future."

They clinked glasses before Hendrick took a strong gulp of his.

"What do you suggest for damage control?"

Geoffrey faced the window and looked outside, taking a moment to collect his thoughts. He took a sip of bourbon, turning to face Hendrick.

"Africa."

"Excuse me?"

"I've looked into some options and we need huge PR points right now. Not only that but Africa needs people to help build a school and a hospital in one of its most impoverished places."

"And this is going to work?"

"Brilliantly. We are going to give them a ton of money while you are going to fly there and get your hands dirty to show the world what your company really stands for."

"After this mess, it's the least I can do."

"Good, because you leave on Monday."

If you enjoyed this other sample, look for **Suspicion by Shyla Starr.**

Also by this Author:

<u>The Prodigal Family: The Abbotts</u>

From the Author

If you enjoyed any of my books then please share the love and promote my books in Amazon.

If you write me a review and send me an email I will send you a free book, or many.
(Just know that these emails are filtered by my publisher.)

Good news is always welcome.

One Last Thing, For Kindle Readers...

When you turn the page, Kindle will give you the opportunity to rate this book and share your thoughts on Facebook and Twitter. If you enjoyed my writings, would you please take a few seconds to let your friends know about it? Because... when they enjoy they will be grateful to you and so will I.

Thank You!

An Open Letter from Just Plain Bob

A message for those who like my stories, those who hate my stories, those who are indifferent and those who have yet to make up their minds.

I have often stated that I really don't care what others think about my stories, that I write for my own enjoyment and then I offer to share. If you like my stories fine and if you don't, also fine since I have already satisfied my target audience - me!

It is human nature to strive to get better. If you take up bowling your first games are going low scoring, but you will work and practice to get better and as your average climbs you may forget the game where you had three gutter balls and shot an eighty-six, but that game is still there in your past.

Your first time on the golf course you shot an eighty on the front nine, but did you settle for that being your game or did you work to improve? You may eventually get a three handicap, but that nine hole eighty is still there as part of your past.

When you hired in at your job did you say, "Cool, I got it made" and do nothing more than what you barely had to do or did you go to work thinking that, "Someday I'm going to be running this place." You might never climb that high, but human nature says that you are going to at least try.

It is the same with authors who write stories and post them on sites like Literotica. Their first stories might not be all that good, but comments and feedback along with a desire to get better drive them toward putting out a better product or to at least try.

I'm no different. My first stories might not have been all that great, but they are still there on the hard drive. I like cheating wife stories and five years ago I found my first adult site that catered to cheating wife stories. It was a pay site, but it had a policy of giving a free lifetime membership to anyone who submitted five stories to the site. How hard can that be I said to myself as I sat down and fired up the word processor and went to work.

I sent my five stories in and sat back to enjoy my free membership and a funny thing happened. I started getting feedback, most of it positive, and I became hooked. I started cranking out more stories. The site I was sending my stories to had seven categories:

Bisexual
Cream Pie
Groups

I Watch
Gang Bang
Racial
SM/BD

I know nothing about bisexual or SM/BD and I had no interest in Groups so all the stories I wrote I tailored for the four remaining categories:

Cream Pie
I Watch
Gang Bang
Racial.

I turned out eight stories a month, two for each category, which means that after five years I have over 120 stories in each of those categories and they are all still on the hard drive.

A year ago I received an email asking me why I never posted stories on Literotica. The answer? I didn't know about Lit. I pulled it up, liked what I saw, and started sending in stories to it. All new stories? No, not hardly, not with over 400 stories sitting on the hard drive. Maybe one new story for each fifteen or so old ones. The newer ones are better, at least I think they are and I have received some feedback that leads me to believe that others think so too, and I will continue to write new ones.

But I am still going to recycle what is on the hard drive, stories that were written specifically to fit the four categories. That means that those of you who hate cream pie stories still have eighty or so to look forward to. Ditto for those who call me a racist; you will get another seventy or so interracial stories.

Those who hate wimps will only see about fifty more of those because the stories I sent to the I Watch category were split 50/50 between what some call wimps and some call "real men." Why the 50/50 split? It came from listening to the readers. I would get feedback asking me why all the men in my stories were hard asses. "In real life men are more forgiving, especially if it is the first indiscretion." So I would write stories with forgiving husbands and boyfriends and then the next batch of feedback would say, "Why are all your husbands spineless wimps" and I'd write stories that went back the other way.

Eventually I came to realize that I was wasting my time - there was no way I could write a story that would satisfy everybody and that is when I adopted my philosophy of writing for my own enjoyment and then offering to share.

As far as the gangbang stories? Well, what can I say? Gangbangs are gangbangs and there are still eighty or so of them to go.

The bottom line is that Literotica readers are going to see more of my old stories than my new ones. If I'm still around three or four years from now it will probably go the other way, more new than old.

I feel the need to respond to some of the comments and emails I have received. By far the largest percentage comes from people who say, "You are an asshole because all women are not whores and sluts and that's all you make them out to be."

Next most common is, "You must really hate women you sick fuck."

"You must be a wimp because all the men in your stories are wimps" is up there in the top ten along with, "Why don't you give it a rest and go crawl off in a hole somewhere."

There is a lot more, but I'm only going to address those four and in reverse order.

I won't stop and go crawl in a hole because I am enjoying the hell out of what I am doing and remember what I said, I am doing this for MY OWN ENJOYMENT and then I offer to share. Some obviously like my sharing with them and so I will continue to do so. No one is holding a gun to a reader's head and telling them they must click on a Just Plain Bob story or die. It is a conscious choice on the reader's part to move that mouse and click on that story.

When a man finds out he has a cheating wife or girlfriend there are only a limited number of ways he can handle it. If he loves her he can forgive, try to forget and try to hold on and somehow make things work. He can turn his back on her, walk away and get on with his life. The third option is to take revenge.

According to a good portion of those who send me feedback the first and second options are proof that the men are wimps. If the man takes the third option he is still considered a wimp if he doesn't do some sort of physical damage to the woman and her lover. These readers believe that the only way not to be a wimp is to kill, maim and destroy everything in sight. Doing that however, will invariably get the man throw in jail and that is why it so rarely happens in real life.

In real life most revenge takes place in the man's head when he says to himself, "I should have _____ (fill in the blank) the fucking cunt!" I know this because I have been there and done that (see The Dark Trilogy). In my stories I try to mirror real life so kill, maim and destroy are going to be for the most part absent. Outside of some fisticuffs there will be very little physical violence in my stories. Most of my husbands are going to do what I did, what several of my friends and others that I know have done, forgive, or walk away. If this makes them wimps and me a wimp for writing the story that way, so be it.

Next is the "I must hate all women." Nothing could be farther from the truth. I love women. I lust after women. I even like whores and sluts. I have been married four times, engaged two other times (that did not end in marriage) and I have always had girlfriends between marriages. My philosophy is that women were put on this earth for me to enjoy and I'm not talking just sexually. I could sit at the mall (and have) for hours and just girl watch.

The engagements, girlfriends and three of the four marriages bring me to the #1 anti JPB comment on the list.

"You are an asshole because all women aren't whores and sluts."

Well dear reader, you can not prove that by me! I will say up front that I KNOW all women aren't whores and sluts, BUT the majority of the women in my life were. My mother ran around on my father for years while he was driving a truck for a living. My Aunt Margaret cheated regularly on my Uncle Bill, as did my Aunt Mildred on my Uncle Paul. My Aunt Betty fucked around on my Uncle Bob for years and finally left him for his brother, my Uncle Wendell. Uncle Wendell in turn caught her on her knees at his company Christmas party giving Season's Greetings to his boss.

My sister is three times divorced and each divorce came about when the then current husband caught her out spreading pollen. Both of the engagements I mentioned ended when I found out that I was not the one and only and a lot of the girls I dated between marriages never made it to engagement status for the same reason.

And that brings me to my three ex-wives. The first one, Helen (I believe I commented on her in the intro to The Dark Trilogy) had seven different lovers before I found out what was going on. I was living proof that love is blind. Ditto with my second wife. She had a secret life that she hid from me and when I found out about her brother, his friends and the gangbangs she was history.

My third marriage ended in divorce because of a different kind of cheating (and I can just imagine the outrage I am going to get over this) - she cheated on me with an idea. I was away from home on business, she was lonely, a couple of Jehovah's Witnesses knocked on the door and my wife, with nothing better to do invited them in. When I came home from my trip I found out that she had found God. On a scale that runs from TRUE BELIEVER on one end to ATHEIST on the other you will find me just to the right of AGNOSTIC and since I would not allow myself to be SAVED the marriage eventually died.

So yes, I write about sluts and whores because as everyone knows, you tend to write about the things you know. And I do like sluts and whores, just not the ones that lie to me and cheat on me.

So be forewarned - if you click on a Just Plain Bob story you will be getting sluts, whores and husbands who do not kill, maim and destroy. There are other things you will rarely find in a Just Plain Bob story. Even though I try to mirror real life my stories all take place in StoryLand. In StoryLand STDs and unwanted pregnancies do not exist unless the author feels like they may add something to the story. Bad things do not happen in StoryLand unless the author so wills it and no amount of "You should have…" in comments and feedback will change a story already posted.

Lastly, I will touch on a truth. None of what I have written here means shit because the same readers will still read the same stories that they profess to hate and make the same comments they have always made. Knowing this, I will deliberately post stories that will have them frothing at the mouth.

It is the least I can do for an adoring public.

Thank you!

Just Plain Bob
justplainbob@awesomeauthors.org